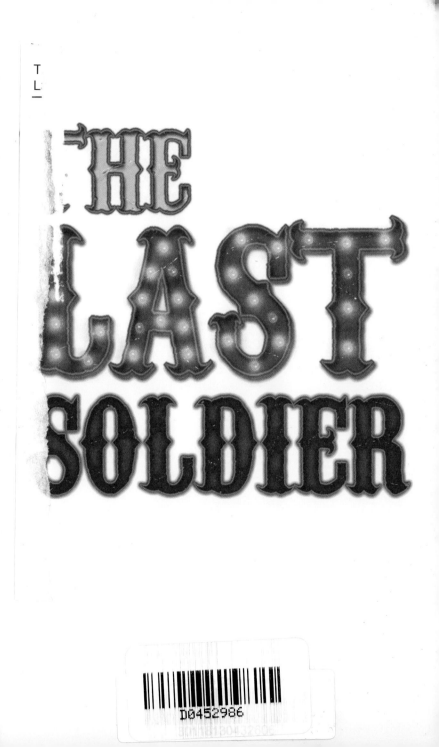

THE
LAST
SOLDIER

THE LAST SOLDIER

Keith Gray

Barrington Stoke

For Clara in the future

First published in 2015 in Great Britain by
Barrington Stoke Ltd
18 Walker Street, Edinburgh, EH3 7LP

www.barringtonstoke.co.uk

Text © 2015 Keith Gray

A CIP catalogue record for this book is available
from the British Library upon request

ISBN: 978-1-78112-439-0

Printed in China by Leo

CONTENTS

CHAPTER 1

THE CARNIVAL ARRIVES

It was the hottest day of the summer when
Captain Tom Peacock's American Amazements
rolled into town. But it was 1922 and every day
that year was hotter than the Devil's own frying
pan.

Me and Joe felt like sizzling, spitting sausages
just about ready to split our skins. We were
swimming in the slow river out behind the old
Mitchum farm. The water there is deep and cool.
The river banks are steep and the trees on the
farm side are tall, wild and shady. It was a good
place to fish for crawdaddies – that's what we
called crayfish in these parts. Joe reckoned they
were easy to catch at this spot. I guess they liked
the shade too.

This day was too hot even to fish and so we'd
spent all morning just lolling and bickering. Joe

wouldn't stop on about how drop-dead bored he was. But he perked right up when he saw the carnival convoy trundling along the road.

"Look, Wade," he shouted. "Will you just look at that?"

The long line of trucks kicked up dust clouds as they rolled by. They were heading for the Mitchums' spare field. Even with all that dust we could see the strings of coloured bulbs ready to be lit. The bright canvas ready to be unfurled. And the bits and pieces ready to become whizzing, spinning rides. That line of trucks was a promise of excitement and music and crowds and laughter. Things our one-horse East Texas town of Lansdale never got to see much of.

Me and Joe stood and gawped.

"Now that's what I call a proper birthday present," Joe said at last. It was his 15th birthday that day. "Ferris wheel, ghost train, whirligig." He counted them off on his fingers in the order he was going to enjoy them. He saved the best for last.

"The Museum of Marvels too," I said. "I gotta see that again."

Joe frowned at me. "Come on, Wade," he said. "That ain't even a thing. Is it?"

"Last time it was," I said. "Don't you remember? Didn't I tell you how scary it was? There was a wolfman they'd hunted and a mermaid they'd caught. They even had a baby dragon too. You must remember."

Joe rolled his eyes at me. The older he got, the more he did that.

"None of them's real," he said. "It's just another con. That baby dragon? Reckon it was probably some ugly old alligator. They just stuffed it and stuck painted chicken wings on its back. Everybody knows there's no such thing as a dragon. Or a wolfman or a mermaid." He smirked at me. "Everyone old enough knows."

I didn't care what Joe said. They'd looked real and true to me. That wolfman with his clawed fingers and snarling teeth. Scariest thing I'd ever seen. And the half-naked mermaid with her hair like tumbling seaweed. I'd had dreams about her.

"You reckon Mama will let us go?" I said to Joe.

Joe's face fell at the thought she might not. "Why shouldn't she?" he said. "Why say that, Wade? It's my birthday, she has to." He splashed at the river, angry like.

"It'll cost money," I said. "And Mama already got you your new shoes." Truth is, I was jealous of my brother's new shoes.

"She didn't buy them," Joe said. "They used to be Pa's." And as he said it, his skinny chest puffed out and his sun-smacked cheeks turned red with pride. For him, the fact they'd been our pa's shoes made them worth more than any money.

They were Sunday-best shoes, not walking shoes, but Joe had wanted to wear them today no matter what. They must have baked his feet, but he'd not complained once as we'd walked here.

I hoped the shoes would be mine too one day, if Joe's feet got too big for them. I'd never had a real pair of shoes. Only the sandals Mama made me from worn-out tyres.

Around these parts it proved how grown-up you were if you had your own pair of proper shoes. I already reckoned I was grown-up enough, but because Joe was the eldest he'd got Pa's old shoes first. That's why I was trying to make him see that he could save wearing the shoes out. I'd told him he should keep them for special. That way they might still be in a half-decent state when they got passed down my way. I knew a brand-new pair of shoes just for me was probably the biggest day-dream of all.

Now the shoes were up in the grass on the bank, staying dry with our clothes.

We stood with the water up to our middles and counted as many as a dozen trucks in the carnival convoy. A handful of cars too. The long line of them stretched all along the old road. Right at the back there was a clown on a motorbike that coughed and puttered along. He wore pants with white, green and blue stripes, and shoes that were as long and flat as boat paddles. His big nose was tomato red, tomato round. He wobbled and weaved in and out of the haze of dust.

I could hear someone laughing. At first I thought it was in my head, like I was looking forward to the carnival so much I was imagining it. I could get like that sometimes. Mama called me a day-dreamer, and she was right. It was like my imagination was too big for its boots sometimes. But the laughing I could hear was real. And it wasn't fun neither, but sharp and nasty.

When I saw who it was, I wished I was dreaming. Joe swore when he saw them too.

Caleb Cubb was the nastiest piece of work in Lansdale, and he was standing on the river bank a little upstream from us. He had his friend Sonny Collins with him. Sonny was the second nastiest piece of work in Lansdale. The two of them were standing side by side and I was so shocked at what they were doing that my mouth swung open wider than a cellar door.

Joe swore again.

Caleb and Sonny were pissing into the river. Honest to God they were! They stood with their peckers in their hands and their backs bent, and their yellow piss made a big arc right out into the river.

It took me and Joe two full seconds to think about how they were upstream. And us downstream.

We splashed and scrambled for the bank.

CHAPTER 2
TROUBLE COME DOWN

Caleb and Sonny were laughing fit to bust a gut. Me and Joe stood and dripped on the river bank. I hoped it was only river water in the pool at my feet.

I was ready to bolt.

"Let's just go," I said to Joe. "Come on."

"I'm older than them now," Joe said. "I ain't afraid of neither of them."

But I saw him itch at his arm as he said it. It was as if he could still feel the ghost of a twinge from when Caleb had stamped on it last year. The arm got busted like a fallen branch. Left it bent and hinky at the elbow. Joe still struggled to lift anything heavy with that arm.

Joe watched Caleb and Sonny trample over the dry grass and the bushes along the river bank to get to us. His hate for Caleb was like a wasp in a jar. I could feel the buzzing inside of him. Trapped and angry.

"Why you wanting to start a fight?" I said. "It's your birthday."

I knew I could high-tail it without him. I knew I could dodge whatever trouble Caleb and Sonny were bringing with them. But I stood there.

Joe might not have needed me. He was three years older than me. But I stood there anyway and watched Caleb and Sonny get closer.

Caleb was ugly enough to make cats yowl. He looked like he had big, rotten peanuts under the skin around his nose and chin. But his daddy was rich and he always dressed fine. His shirt was blue check with shiny buttons like silver coins that glinted in the sun. It looked new. Proper new. Not hand-me-down.

Caleb didn't come right up to us but kept a step or two away. Maybe he was scared we'd push him in the river if he got too close. Scared to get his fine shirt wet.

Sonny wasn't dressed so fine – he looked like a scarecrow had worn his clothes first. His thick red hair was so greasy you could probably fry eggs and bacon right there on his head. I reckoned soap was the only thing that ever scared Sonny. He was laughing at us as he followed behind Caleb.

Caleb held up a hand to shade his eyes and squinted at us in the bright sunshine. "What you doing this side of the river?" he said. "I know I already told you before. This is my daddy's land this side."

Joe made a big act of looking all around. He shrugged. "Is that right?" he said. "Last I knew it was still Old Man Mitchum's farm."

"Maybe for now it is," Caleb said. "But not for too long any more. Old Man Mitchum's on his last legs, so I hear. Soon as he's pushing up daisies this is all gonna be my daddy's. Every flat inch of it." He took a step closer to us. "And like I've told you before, I'm not happy you being on it."

Caleb's pa's farm was the biggest in the county – acres and acres of fields of beet and corn. These past years it had eaten up two more farms over to the east and now looked set to gobble up Old Man Mitchum's land too. Caleb's pa was a big, hunched man who didn't speak much. Never laughed neither. He was as grizzly as a bear with a hangover. The rumour was if he ever caught his workers stealing from him he'd sew them up in a bed sheet and drop them in the river. Both him and Caleb had tiny eyes like dead pebbles.

"Reckon you ought to get to swimming back across that side," Sonny said. He pointed to the trees on the far bank. "Yessir, that's what I reckon. Get back over there, y'hear?"

Sonny chummed with Caleb because no one else would. And the same was true the other way. They weren't friends. Caleb just liked having someone he could lord it over and boss around. Sonny liked the stuff Caleb gave him sometimes – stolen dirty pictures of girls, and fancy cookies from New York or Chicago.

Sonny lived with his four older brothers and four older sisters on the far side of town. Their knackered shack stood in a part of town Mama wouldn't let me and Joe go, near the railroad junction. The gossips in the town said Sonny's pa had been in prison for over a year when Sonny was born. No way was he Sonny's real pa. Maybe that was why he beat Sonny so much. Some days Sonny walked proper hinky because his pa had used the buckle of his belt to whip him. I reckoned Sonny might be glad his pa was in prison again just now. This time it was for thieving sacks of coal from a passing train.

Joe stood up taller. He was shorter than Caleb but he kept his shoulders square. "Old Man Mitchum and our pa are friends," he said. "He lets us come here anytime we like. Maybe it's you two shouldn't be here."

Sonny just went and sat himself down on the bank. He let his bare, grubby feet dangle in the slow water and grinned up at Caleb. "I gone and got all settled now," he said. "I don't want Joe's pa to catch me, y'hear? Yessir, I reckon I surely would hate that to happen."

"Honest, Joe. We swear, yeah?" Caleb said. "Me and Sonny swear. If your pa comes along right now, right this minute, we'll scarper. You won't see us for dust."

And they laughed like wolves on a turkey farm.

It bit me deep. But that laughter with its sharp teeth was too much for Joe. He jumped at Caleb.

I tried to grab him, but he was too fast. Too fast for Caleb, too. Joe shoved and punched and battered at Caleb, and he knocked him back. He went on pushing and shoving and whaling on him.

Sonny scrambled to get to his feet. I knew I could keep out of it, but Joe couldn't fight both of them. Not with his crooked elbow and weak arm. So I yelled and ran at Sonny, windmilling my fists.

He swatted me away like I was a bug. I went face first into the river.

Before I'd even managed to get my feet under me and my head up out of the water, my brother landed with a splash in beside me.

I reckon all that laughing from Caleb and Sonny hurt me and Joe almost as much as their punches. Joe swore and cursed at them so bad that Mama's hair would have turned crispy if she'd heard him. She would never think he even knew such words.

"Stay off my daddy's land," Caleb shouted when he stopped with his laughing. He hooked a thumb over his shoulder. "And see that carnival? I'm telling you now, that's on my daddy's land too."

I was scared Joe might want to stay and fight. But Sonny chucked a rock that missed us by a kitten's whisker. Then Caleb was hurling rocks and lumps of mud too. We waded and stumbled our way across to the bank on the far side as fast as we could.

As soon as Joe had climbed out he shouted back over at them. "You can't stop us from going to the carnival."

"You'll get worse if we catch you there." Caleb shouted back. "You hear me? I'll bust both your arms this time."

Joe snatched up his new shoes out of the grass. "You'll have to bust my arms and legs and my neck too before you stop me going."

"Maybe I'll do just that," Caleb shouted. "You just see if I don't."

CHAPTER 3
PROMISES AND THREATS

We walked home under the afternoon sun. It was so hot it felt heavy on our backs. Joe didn't want to talk. He clomped along in Pa's old shoes – his new shoes – with his head down and his hair in his eyes.

I'd asked him if he wanted to play Blind Man's Walk. It was a game we used to play a lot. You had to close your eyes tight shut and walk all the way home like that. But asking him if he wanted to play only seemed to make his mood darker still.

"Can it, Wade," he told me. "It's a game for little kids. It's easier than catching a cold in winter." And he rubbed at his hinky elbow as if it hurt.

Home was two rooms above Gunther's Barber Shop on Wood Street. Mr Gunther had his own house all to himself on Cooper Street. Ma often said how good he'd been to us these past few years. Pa used to work for Mr Gunther and I remember sitting in the big chair with the snip-snip-snip of Pa's scissors close to my ears as he cut my hair. Pa sometimes let me have a splash of hair tonic too, and I used to pretend it smelled of something nasty every time. Maybe one time like horse-pucky stew, another time like a rattlesnake's bathwater. It always used to make us laugh.

Joe wasn't so keen on Mr Gunther, but I liked him OK. He was balder than a shaved egg, which was mighty funny for a barber. He cut my hair these days and he was much stingier with the tonic than Pa had been. But he made up for it with his books. He kept a stack of dime novels for his customers to read while they waited on their haircuts, and he let me read them too. On those slow days when there were no customers we'd sit side by side in the big chairs and read about gunslingers' ghosts and daring explorers.

But what Mr Gunther loved most of all was to talk, and I reckoned a lot of what he told me was real interesting. Almost all the men in town came to his shop and Mr Gunther told the best gossip about them. Funny stories that weren't for polite company. Joe said Mr Gunther's gossip was plain dull, nothing but small talk about small-town people in a small-minded town.

He'd say, "My name's Joseph Harper Junior. I ain't never changing it."

Joe's name was the reason for the big fight between Joe and Caleb outside of the school two winters back. It started because Caleb called Joe "Joseph Gunther Junior" and wouldn't let up. And it ended with Joe's broken arm.

We didn't tell Mama what happened. Joe told her he'd fallen out of a tree and he made me swear to keep his secret. But I didn't like secrets. And I didn't like the way Joe forced me to choose whose side I was on. Mama's or his.

The stairs that go up to our rooms are around the back of the barber shop. Mr Gunther had painted them only the week before, but Joe and I had already scratched our names into the wood again. When we got home that day after the fight at the river, Joe threw himself down on the bottom step with a grunt.

"We're not gonna tell Mama, OK?" he said.

I shrugged. "OK."

"Don't go blabbing, Wade," he said. "She don't need to know."

"OK," I said again. I fidgeted in the hot sun. Another secret.

"I ripped his shirt," Joe said.

He held up two things that looked like coins. But then I saw they were two bright buttons off of Caleb's swanky shirt.

"They popped right off in my hand when I grabbed him," Joe said. "D'you reckon he's gonna make me buy him a new shirt?"

"If he wants you to, he'll have to tell everyone why you were fighting," I said. "And we'll just tell everyone what him and Sonny were doing. I don't reckon he'll want people to know that."

Joe rested his arms on his knees and stared at his shoes. He took out his hanky and wiped the dust from them. "It was what they were saying about Pa. And then laughing so much. It got me so damn mad," he said.

"Me too."

"Pa is gonna come back," Joe said. "You believe that, don't you?"

I didn't know what to say. Now I was the one staring at my feet.

"He is," Joe said. "I know he is. One day. Mama knows it too. That's why she's never agreed to marry Mr Gunther. She's still waiting for Pa."

It was 1917 – five years before – when we said goodbye to Pa. He'd gone to fight the war in Europe. He'd promised us he'd come back when he'd done his duty. The war ended the very next year, but we'd not seen Pa since. No one had.

Mama used to cry at night when she thought we couldn't hear. But we didn't hear her crying so much now. I thought maybe Joe was wrong. Maybe Ma had stopped believing Pa would turn up again one of these days. Maybe it was only Joe who still believed that.

I could see tears in Joe's eyes. Hot tears, bright with anger. "Sonny Collins's pa is a rotten thief, everyone knows it," he said. "And Caleb

Cubb's pa just steals other people's land. It don't matter how much money he's got, that don't mean he's better than us. And I ain't going to let either of them two laugh at our pa."

"But what about the carnival?" I asked. "What about what Caleb said?"

Before Joe could answer, Mama's voice made us both jump.

"I thought I heard you two whispering." She poked her head out of the door at the top of the stairs. "I wasn't expecting you back so soon. But I guess the smell of birthday cake is too much to resist."

Me and Joe stood side by side and did our best not to look guilty. Mama frowned. She must have seen Joe scrub the tears from his eyes and she must have known something was wrong.

But maybe she thought it was best not to hear about any trouble, not when there was a birthday to celebrate. She must have scrimped and scraped to afford butter and sugar and eggs to make Joe's cake.

She stepped out onto the stairs in her apron covered in white puffs of flour. "Don't neither of you want any of this cake I spent half the day baking?" She smiled. "Didn't I tell you it's still warm?" She held the door open and waved us up.

I went to jump up the stairs two at a time.

Joe held me back a second. "We're going to that carnival tonight," he whispered. "I don't give a hot damn about Caleb and his threats. Trouble might just come down on him for once. That's a promise."

CHAPTER 4
BRIGHT LIGHTS

That birthday cake tasted like heaven. I told Mama so. In fact, I was extra nice about it since Joe hardly said a word. Mama tried talking to him, but he'd only answer with a shrug or a "suppose so". I wanted to tell Mama it wasn't her fault. It was Caleb Cubb who'd gotten under my brother's skin like a blood-sucking tick.

But I kept my promise to Joe. I didn't say a word about that afternoon and just acted extra happy to make up for his funk.

The first time Joe strung a sentence together was when he asked if we could go to the carnival that night.

Mama frowned. "I don't like carnivals," she said. "All that sparkle and glitter washes off in the rain, you know. I've never trusted anything about them."

"But Mama ..." Joe began.

"They don't treat their animals right," Mama went on. "Poor things look half-starved cooped up in their cages. And the people don't even treat each other right if you believe the stories you hear. Mr Gunther says they'd swindle a dollar off a dead man."

"Pa would let us go if he was here," Joe said.

Part of me thought that was a horrible thing for Joe to say. Another part was glad because it made Mama change her mind.

She kept her purse in a dull and dented coffee tin on the top shelf in the kitchen. The way she dug in that purse made me wonder how deep down her last few coins were. But she smiled at the hug Joe gave her to say thanks. She told us to be home no later than an hour after it got dark and waved as we ran away up the road. She'd given us a dime and a nickel each. I loved her for giving me the same as Joe when it wasn't my birthday.

Even before we reached the river and the Mitchums' farm we could hear the hoots and whistles of music on the breeze. The tune was "Bronco Billy Rag". It led us across the bridge and at Hay Street Bend we joined a straggle of townsfolk who were all heading the same way.

We walked faster, threading among the crowd. The bustle and noise drew us like a magnet, stronger and stronger the closer we got. Joe's mood was lifting too. He wasn't rubbing at his elbow no more. He grinned at me, and his eyes were bright and excited.

I'd been worried the carnival would never get set up in one day. But now we could see the strings of jewel-coloured lights all around the field.

"They look like happy stars, don't they, Joe?" I said.

Joe rolled his eyes at me and my embarrassment shut me up. But it was true. In the light of the setting sun, I reckoned that was just how all those twinkling bulbs looked.

I remembered what Mama had said about carnivals, but many of the Lansdale folk didn't seem to agree. Maybe they just didn't care.

The Mitchums' field was a buzzing, bustling maze of tents and lights and rides and corndog stands. Everything around me felt like it was brimming over with colour and movement and noise and smells. It was too much to take in at once. I stood in the middle of it all as it spun and whirled and shouted and blazed around me.

The Strongest Man in Texas would wrestle me for a dime. The Bearded Lady would kiss me. And Dr Lucker would sell me his World Famous Super Cure in a bottle. Even I knew it was just Coca-Cola and whiskey mixed, but I saw Preacher Blake buy a whole crate-load.

If Caleb and Sonny were there, we didn't see sight nor sign of them. I think we both forgot about them.

Joe had also forgotten his plan of what things to do and see in what order and now he wanted to try his skill on the shooting shy first. He was a real good aim most of the time, and he was cross when he missed the tin ducks first time around. Then he was angry when he missed them for a second time. The skinny guy on the stall chewed on his cigar and pushed his hat off his eyes. He egged Joe on with promises of prizes if he tried just one more time. I pointed out to Joe that he'd already spent his nickel. At this rate, he'd spend all his money before we'd been at the carnival half an hour.

"Pa taught me how to shoot," Joe said. "I'm good. You know I should of got them goddam ducks, don't you?"

The guy cocked a brow at Joe's cussing.

"I was just warming up," Joe told him. "Your goddam gun's crooked!"

We ran rabbit before the guy could get his hands on us.

We dodged and weaved among the crowds to the Ferris wheel. We paid and climbed into the rocking seat side by side, and let it swing us up. High, high, high.

From the top of the wheel the town looked so small. Like I could gather it up in my arms. Or maybe sweep the whole lot behind the hills. I loved that we could see everything, and that we knew everything we could see. The schoolhouse, Chapman's Pond, Main Street, Wood Street …

"That's Mr Gunther's shop, see?" I told Joe. "So that's our rooms, right?" I waved as if Mama might see us.

But Joe's mood darkened. "Don't you hate that everything's so small?" he said. "Maybe that's why Pa hasn't come back yet. I'm getting to think I don't blame him."

Joe said the Museum of Marvels was too babyish for him, so after the Ferris wheel let us back down to earth, I went looking for it by myself. I reckoned Joe was going back along to the shooting shy to lose the rest of his money.

It took me a while to find what I was looking for. It was right at the very far edge of the Mitchums' field, right above the steep river bank. There was no crowd here. And it was almost dark. It was about as far from the noise and buzz of the rest of the carnival as you could get.

CHAPTER 5
INSIDE THE MUSEUM

The Museum was a long, low truck trailer perched on top of the high river bank. It looked like one good push might send it crashing and sliding all the way down into the water. The outside was painted with pictures of the Marvels that were to be found inside. Maybe the pictures had been bright once, a long time ago. They were faded now. Even in the dim light I could see the paint was flaking away. It made me remember what Mama had said about the carnival's sparkle washing off in the rain. And maybe I would have turned back, gone to find Joe again, but someone was watching me.

An old woman smoking a stinky cigar sat on the short steps that led up to the door. She was dressed in flouncy skirts of red and gold. Her heavy gold ear-rings dragged her lobes into baggy loops. She must have been twice as old as

Mama, but she had a tiny baby in her arms. The baby sucked on the old woman's little finger like it was a bottle. They both watched me walk up.

"Is it open?" I asked. I felt very far away from the carnival crowds. Maybe part of me wanted her to say it was closed.

"Don't you think you're a tad too tiddly for this?" the old woman asked. Her voice was not from around Lansdale. She hooked a thumb over her shoulder. "Were you not told? These things? Well, they can give young 'uns terrible nightmares."

"I saw them last time," I said. "And I don't get no nightmares."

It was almost true. I didn't get nightmares now.

The old woman looked at me for a good long time. The baby was staring at me too with its little dark eyes. I couldn't look back at both of them together. So I looked at the paintings on the side of the trailer.

"The wolfman," I said, and I pointed at him. "He was my favourite. Have you still got him?"

"Mmm-hmm, was he?" The old woman chucked the baby under its chin. Her fingernails were cracked and brown, but the baby squirmed with pleasure. Then the old woman sighed and held out her hand for my money. "Did I tell you we've a couple of new Marvels?" she asked. "Since last time we came past this way?"

She took my nickel and didn't offer any change.

"You'll remember to yell out real loud?" she said. "If you get too scared?"

She shuffled her bottom to one side of the wooden steps to let me pass by. I went as fast as I could. I didn't want her to think I was yellow. And I didn't want to touch her as I went past.

At the top of the steps was a heavy red curtain. The old woman had turned to watch me, so I pushed it to one side and went straight in. It was as dark and close as the Devil's back pocket. I stood to let my eyes get used to the gloom. Then I shuffled forward.

There was a narrow corridor along the middle of the trailer with the Marvels on both sides. I was going to have to walk all the way in between them to get out the exit door at the other end. Some of the marvels were in glass cases. Others were behind a low, sagging rope. The light bulbs overhead glowed red then green then blue, and back again.

I didn't like that I was alone here. If I held my breath I could hear the muffled far away sounds of the rest of the carnival.

The display on my left was called "Attacked by Vampire Bats". Behind the glass was a man crouched down on his knees. His mouth was wide and scared. He held his hands above his head to fend off a swarm of bats on strings.

There was a hand-written sign to one side of the display. I had to squint in the gloom to read it.

"These night-time horrors come from the jungles of the darkest Amazon. They have needle-sharp teeth and a terrifying lust for blood. The people of the Amazon say they can drain a grown man dry of every drop of his blood in less than an hour. These little devils have been seen in local woodlands of late. Mind to be watchful as you walk home tonight."

The man was a waxwork dummy and someone had painted two bloody, dribbling wounds on his neck. Vampire bites.

I couldn't tell if the bats were real, or as fake as a crocodile's smile. I got as close to the glass as I could. I peered up at the bats on their strings. The light went from red to green to blue and I saw their tiny eyes glitter. I jumped back.

Then I laughed at myself for being a chump. I rolled my eyes like Joe did, just in case the old woman was peering in at me through a peephole somewhere. I scratched the back of my neck, as if I could feel her stare prickling at me there.

The wolfman was on the other side. My favourite, so I'd said.

The wolfman was frozen mid-howl – his head thrown back to look at the moon painted above him. Grasping claws, snarling teeth. He was naked but for a tatty cloth to hide his pecker. But he was also covered head to toe in thick, black hair. The sign on this display said he'd been hunted down in the wilds of Canada. It said it had taken 20 daring hunters and brave lumberjacks to capture him. But as I looked at him I saw a clump of fur was missing from the side of his mouth. And there was something about the way his mouth was open. And the way his head was tilted.

I looked back at the waxwork dummy and the vampire bats. It was the exact same mouth. On the exact same face. One scared, the other scary. But the same. The wolfman was the exact same dummy, just dressed up different.

It wasn't real or true at all. It was monkey-shine. Horse-pucky. Just like Joe had told me.

I wondered if the old woman was chomping her cigar and laughing at me out there on the steps. She had my nickel in the pocket of her flouncy skirts.

The mermaid was even worse. Her long fish-tail was falling apart, and there was sawdust leaking out. One side of her wax face looked like it had gotten too hot on its summer journey. Her glass eye had slipped in its socket and was half way down her painted cheek. It was staring at the floor.

I was so embarrassed and sick at heart with myself for being so foolish and young that I turned away from the baby dragon in the next display. I just didn't want to look at it. Joe would be right about that too. I walked along to the exit. I didn't want to be taken for a fool any more. I stamped as I went, making angry echoes inside the trailer that I hoped the old woman would hear over the carnival noise.

But the very last glass cabinet caught my eye. I stopped, trapped by his stare.

"The Last Solider."

CHAPTER 6
THE LAST SOLDIER

He was sitting in a chair right up close to the glass. A soldier in full uniform with a rifle across his lap. His mouth open wide, wide. Screaming.

It wasn't a false scream. Not like the dummy wolfman or the waxwork man the bats were attacking. This scream was lips peeled back from teeth, eyes bulging, terrified. Pain stretched the skin on his face as he cried out.

The Last Soldier looked very real.

I couldn't stop staring at him. I leaned towards the glass but I didn't touch it. Was I just being young and foolish again? I couldn't see any paint smudges and he didn't look like rubbed-smooth wax. His flesh was like pale stretched leather. It was tight across his forehead and nose, yet his cheeks were sunk and shadowed.

He sat there silently screaming, screaming, screaming at me.

I took a step away from the glass. My own skin prickled with chills.

And then I saw the bullet hole. His chest had a blackened hole as big as the nickel I'd paid to come in here. A deadly hole punched through a uniform perfect in every other way.

I looked from the bullet hole to his face. I wanted to run, but my legs wouldn't move. There was a sign at the bottom of the glass cabinet and I forced myself to take my eyes off the soldier to read it. I bent down and out of the corner of my eye the solider watched me as I did.

"Private Stanley George Jones of the British East Yorkshire Infantry Regiment," I read.

"Private Jones was the last soldier to die in the Great War of 1914–18. He was shot in the heart and killed in Mons, Belgium, at 11:58 p.m., on 10th November 1918. So many men lost their lives in this terrible war that now it is claimed the world will never have to suffer another war like it. So much was lost in the 'war to end all wars' that must never be lost again. Brave men such as Private Jones won freedom for future generations. He is the world's Last Soldier. We salute him."

I was shaking as I stood up again. The Last Soldier sat there, frozen in the moment of his death. I thought of Pa. I thought of Pa waving goodbye. I gripped my hands into fists. The light above the glass cabinet flickered and went off.

Then it flickered on again and everything was flooded in bright blood-red light.

I ran.

The Last Soldier watched me go.

I leaped out of the Museum's exit and stumbled onto the grass. The old woman called after me, something about being careful of nightmares. I ignored her. I couldn't get the soldier's screaming face, terror-filled face, out of my mind. The black hole gaping in his chest.

I ran, and I felt like he was chasing me. I ran and ran until I reached the crowds, where I began to call Joe's name.

Shouts boomed next to me and I cried out, startled. It was just someone winning on the coconut shy. A blast of music exploded overhead. I ducked, cowered. Lights burst around me, blazing, dazzling. People in the crowd charged at me and I ran from them.

I ran to the Ferris wheel again. I needed to be up and out of the chaos around me.

And when I was up high, looking down on the carnival, I felt my heart slow again. I breathed in big gulps of cool night air. I couldn't get the Last Soldier to leave my mind. I saw his face every time I closed my eyes, every time I blinked. But I felt far away from him now. Had he been real or just a painted dummy like the wolfman?

I opened my eyes and looked down on Lansdale again. The houses were dark patches between the lines of street lights. The black, shiny river curled around them. I'd lost track of time but I knew Mama would want Joe and me home very soon. She'd be waiting for us. She'd be worried.

I wondered how much she would worry if her sons ever had to go to war. What must she have felt when Papa went? But maybe we would never need to go. Maybe I really had seen the world's Last Soldier.

As the Ferris wheel rolled, spun and swung me back down to earth again, I looked for Joe among the crowd. I saw a bobbing red head under the lights of the gun shy. Sonny Collins. And the boy standing with him was Caleb Cubb. I saw a third boy on the ground. He was squirming in the dirt, holding his hands over his head. I saw Caleb kick him.

CHAPTER 7
FOLLOWED HOME

I lay awake late, staring up at the dark bedroom ceiling. There was a sliver of moonlight between the curtains. I listened to Joe groan and murmur in his sleep in his bed on the other side of the room. Maybe he was having a bad dream. Maybe he was remembering what had happened at the carnival.

Caleb and Sonny had beaten him bad.

When they were finished with him, Joe had fat, pulpy lips and a bloody, crooked nose. Bruises like evil rainbows of purple and blue and black and yellow ran all down his body. I supposed it was lucky nothing got broken this time. It would have been much worse if it hadn't have been for the guy from the gun stall. He'd leaped over his stall and pulled Sonny and Caleb off of Joe. Then I tried to help Joe stand but he wouldn't let me. He'd stayed curled up in a ball and tried to hide his tears. People gathered to stare like he was one of the marvels in the phony museum. I was so relieved when Mr Gunther pushed his way past the crowds and helped me carry Joe home to our rooms above his barber shop.

Mama had been beside herself. She snatched and grabbed all sorts of creams and tonics and salves from her medicine box. But Joe would have none of it. He climbed into bed with all his clothes on and pulled the covers tight around him.

He didn't say a word to any of us. He lay in bed and cried himself to sleep.

So I had to tell Mama the full story of what had happened earlier down at the river. And of how I'd been up on the Ferris wheel when I saw Caleb and Sonny beating on Joe. But I said nothing about the Museum of Marvels. It wasn't part of the story. At least, I didn't think so then.

Mama's face ticked with worry. Anger too. On hot summer nights we left the door onto the stairs open to let the cooking heat out and any

welcome breeze in. Mama marched in and out of
the door looking angry one second, anxious the
next. It was like she wanted to run somewhere,
but knew she never could. At last she sat down
at the table and clasped her hands in front of
her.

"Should I say something to Marshall Cubb?"
she asked Mr Gunther. Marshall Cubb was
Caleb's father. "Should I go see him?" Mama
went on. "Tell him what his son has done to my
son?"

Mr Gunther had a smear of Joe's blood on
his clean shirt. "Maybe I should go," he said.
"Marshall might take it better from a man."

Mama shook her head at this and chewed on
her lip. But she knew it was true. "Won't want a
woman dressing him down, you think?"

So Mr Gunther set off to ride out to the Cubb
farm and Mama asked me to tell her all that had
happened again, even when it was clear it hurt
her to hear it.

"Mama?" I asked. "Why is Caleb so cruel?"

"I think he wants to be just like his daddy," she told me. "He believes his daddy got to be as rich as he is because he's mean. But not every mean man is rich. Look at Sonny Collins's daddy. He's meaner than a bucket full of rattlesnakes, but stupid with it. He's never stolen anything but that he got caught. Marshall Cubb is a clever man, for all he's mean. But Caleb can't just up and copy his daddy's brains. It's not as easy to copy brains as it is to copy meanness."

I sat with her at the table. "That's why he's like he is?" I said. "It's all because he wants to be the same as his pa?"

She nodded. "Wants to follow in his daddy's footsteps. A lot of boys do."

I thought about it. "Do I?" I asked.

"I don't think you got to know your daddy well enough," Mama said. "Maybe if you'd had a couple more years with him. Maybe then."

I was careful with my next question. "What was my pa like?" I asked.

Mama closed her eyes as if that would help her remember. She breathed deep. I was scared she might cry again. But then she got a small smile – a half-smile – on her face.

"Easy to laugh, but not always happy," she said. "Stubborn but kind when he needed to be. Handsome. Brimming over with fancy ideas and restless with it. He always looked further than the horizon instead of at the spot where he stood."

"Like Joe?" I asked.

And now there were tears in Mama's eyes again. "Perhaps."

I wanted to stop her crying, so I smiled at her. "I could be more like Pa and Joe," I said. But I reckon that just made it worse.

"Oh, you're more than enough like your pa for me, Wade," Mama said. "You've got his wild ideas and big imagination, I know that much. And I worry about what happens when sons follow fathers, and grandfathers. If that keeps on year after year then nothing will ever change, will it? There'll never be an ending to anything. Just more of the same, on and on."

She dabbed at her tears with the hem of her apron, then she looked me square in the eyes. "Follow your own feet, Wade Harper," she said. "That's my advice. Make your own footprints." Then she chased me to bed.

I lay and stared up at a sliver of moonlight across the bedroom ceiling and listened to Joe wheeze and moan in his sleep. I thought about everything Mama had told me. I thought I understood some of what she had said, if not all of it. And I wondered if Pa ever would come home to us like Joe reckoned.

Maybe it was the thought of Pa that made me look over at the bedroom door, as if he was going to appear there. And my heart leaped. Someone was standing in the shadow of the door. A man. A soldier. But not Pa.

Even in the darkness I could see the screaming face. The stretched skin, the terrified mouth. I could see the uniform. I could see the bullet hole punched in the chest. The Last Soldier watched me from the door. His eyes rolled this way and that. Searching, searching. Then they fixed on me.

I tried to yell. My throat clogged. I struggled to move. My muscles froze. I had to fight to squeeze my eyes shut.

The Last Soldier shuffled a slow step towards me. I heard his army boots drag and scrape across the floor.

At last I cried out. "NO!"

Joe bucked upright in his bed. "What? What's up?" I heard his breath catch as he hurt his bruises. "Wade?" he called.

But the Last Soldier was gone.

"He followed me," I tried to say, but my breath was too ragged. "He followed me home."

Joe sighed. "Keep your bad dreams to yourself," he told me. "Haven't I got a whole heap of my own already?"

And for a long while in that dark night, we lay there in silence, each of us wary of our own bad dreams.

CHAPTER 8
FATHERS AND SONS

I slept fitfully. I dreamed of Pa in a cage. Crowds of people were fighting to look at him. They squabbled and pushed just to catch a glimpse of him. But he was shaking the bars and shouting. "Let me out. I've got to go home. Let me out. I want to go home."

I woke all groggy and sore.

Joe's bed was empty.

I could hear a man's voice in the kitchen and I jumped out of bed with pictures of the Last Soldier flashing in my head. But just as fast I told myself that last night had been nothing but my imagination. The Last Soldier at the door was a bad dream, that was all. Then I recognised the voice as Mr Gunther's. I pulled my clothes on and felt like the biggest bone-headed chump of them all.

I saw Joe's new shoes on the floor under his bed. He'd left them neat and tidy. I crept across the room and tried them on. I was disappointed but not surprised that they were too big for me. So I put them back just as I'd found them, hoping Joe wouldn't notice.

It was another sweltering day. The kitchen smelled of stale coffee and Mama sat with a cup in her hands. She looked dog-tired.

"Do you know where your brother's got to?" Mama asked.

I could only shake my head.

She stared at me like it could be all my fault. "I've got to get myself to work before I'm late," she said.

Mama worked as a maid at the only hotel in Lansdale and we all knew how lucky she was to have any kind of job.

"You'll have to help Mr Gunther in the shop," she said, "since Joe's made himself scarce. But when you do see Joe, you make sure to tell him that he better be home for supper. We need words."

Mama marched out the door and Mr Gunther and I listened as she rushed down the stairs.

"Reckon you'd better follow me," Mr Gunther said.

I grabbed an apple for my breakfast and did as I was told.

The gossip in the barber's shop that morning was all about the carnival. And about Joe's beating. Half the town had seen it happen, or so it seemed. Every customer that came in asked Mr Gunther how Joe was.

"He's a tough lad that one," Mr Gunther told them all as he snipped their shaggy hair or shaved their saggy chins. "He takes after his pa. I just hope he don't think no revenge needs to be done."

I guessed that last part was aimed at me in the hope I'd pass the advice along.

I swept the floor and polished the mirrors. I kept my head down, but I listened to everything that was said.

"I rode out to see Marshall Cubb last night," Mr Gunther told one customer. "Mrs Harper was beside herself and so I told her I'd go. Her Joe was beaten black and bloody. He was a sight, I'm telling you. So I thought I needed to talk to the father man-to-man. And you know what he said? 'Boys will be boys.' That was about the sum of it."

The customer grunted and wrinkled his nose. "Guess you can't blame him for sticking up for kin," he said.

Mr Gunther shrugged. "He even blamed young Joe for starting it," he said. "He went that far."

"That's not how it happened," I burst out.

Mr Gunther and his customer turned to stare at me.

"Joe never started nothing," I said. "And it wasn't a fair fight. It was two on one. Sonny Collins was with Caleb Cubb all the time."

I didn't know the customer's name, but he turned all the way round in the barber's chair and winked at me, friendly-like. "The Collins boy got nabbed pinching from the carnival folks, so I heard," he said. "And no matter the kind of joint they may be running, carney folks don't take well to people stealing off of them. So there's no need to worry about Sonny, my lad. He's keeping his old man company in some jail cell even as we talk."

"Like father, like son," Mr Gunther said.

By noon the shop was quiet. Mr Gunther said now would be a good time for me to go find Joe. But after thinking about Pa so much recently there was something I wanted to ask him first.

"Mr Gunther," I said. "Are you going to marry Mama?"

I surprised him enough to make him stammer. "I'm not sure that's a right and proper thing for us to discuss, young Wade," he said.

"Do you think my pa will come home?" I asked.

"Anyone who knew your pa wishes that with all their heart," Mr Gunther said. "He was an honest man and a good friend. And that's why your mama finds it so hard to believe he won't walk in the door again one of these days. But I'm sure she knows I'm here if she needs me. You and Joe know that too, right?"

I nodded. "Yes, sir," I said. And realised I meant it. I reckoned I could trust Mr Gunther to tell me the truth, so I dared to ask something else. "Why did Pa leave in the first place?" I said.

Mr Gunther thought hard before he answered. "Your pa was a good man, and a decent barber when he put his mind to it," he said. "But he struggled to be a family man sometimes. He told me he'd joined the army so as to burn the adventure out of him. And he believed he'd come back home ready to settle. Happy to just be."

"You don't think Pa will ever come home, do you?" I asked.

Mr Gunther looked at me direct and put his hand on my shoulder. "I think that if he was able to," he said, "your pa would have come home a long time ago."

We stayed like that a moment. Then, before I went to look for Joe, I crawled under the stairs around the back where no one could see me and cried. Just a little, to get the tears out of me and set myself straight.

Then I looked for Joe in all our usual hidey-holes. The treehouse on Copper Street. The old barn at the foot of Given Hill. He wasn't there. So I tried to guess places where he might go instead. But he wasn't in any of those either.

Supper that night was just Mama and me. And the silence made me feel about as nervy as a blind man on a cactus farm.

Joe didn't turn up until I was in bed.

I heard Mama shouting at him, then she scolded him and cried. I listened to her and I understood she had a struggle to be both Ma and Pa to us.

"Where've you been?" I whispered to Joe when he was in his bed across the room from me. "Where you been all day?"

"Back to the carnival," he said.

"Did you go looking for Caleb?"

"No," he said. "I went looking for a way out."

"What's that supposed to mean?" I asked.

In the darkness, I heard him turn his back on me. "Go to sleep," he told me.

But I couldn't. I lay there and pondered and worried in the dark. I heard Joe toss and turn a little. Then I heard him snoring and I was still wide awake.

Wide awake enough to see the terrible figure in the doorway.

CHAPTER 9
THE NIGHTMARE RETURNS

The wide, terror-filled eyes. The mouth stretched in a scream. The Last Soldier stepped out of the shadows. Army boots scraped on the wooden floor. Fear pinned me to my bed. I didn't dare blink. I didn't dare breathe.

The Last Soldier walked into the room. Shuffling. Closer. His rolling eyes searched for something and found me. Dragging his heavy boots. Looming over me. Reaching out a bony, crooked hand. There was black dirt under his broken nails. And I could smell him. He smelled like the crushed, dead dog we once found beside the train tracks. His breath was rotten on my face.

"Joe. Joe, please. Help me," I called out. My throat was thick with choking horror.

Joe muttered, still asleep.

The Last Soldier twisted his head away from me, as if he'd only just noticed my brother in his bed. With jerky, snapping movements, he turned towards Joe. And I saw him from behind for the first time. There was a great, ragged flap in his uniform jacket. A dark, gaping hole in his back. I could see jagged bone where the killing bullet had exploded out of him. It was three – no, four – times the size of the neat hole in his chest.

The Last Soldier staggered towards my sleeping brother. His heavy boots tore and scratched on the floorboards. His head swayed loose on his stick-thin neck.

"Joe," I cried. "Wake up. Joe."

My brother sat bolt upright in bed. He opened his mouth and filled his lungs ready to scream. But the Last Soldier put a hand on my brother's forehead. Just placed his leathery palm against Joe's head and leaned so close that their noses almost touched. Joe's scream never reached his lips.

The Last Soldier spoke to him. I couldn't hear what he said. It was a breathy, whispery hiss of words right into Joe's ear. And Joe just nodded, like he was in a daze.

When I blinked the Last Soldier was gone. Puff. Like a carnival trick. And Joe was fast asleep again.

I was icy cold as I climbed out of bed. I crept across the room to kneel beside Joe. I said his name, loud, twice. Then I shook him awake.

"What?" he grumbled. "Goddammit, Wade. Let me sleep, will you?"

"He was here," I said. "He spoke to you."

Joe flipped his pillow over to the cool side and punched it into shape. "Go to sleep, Wade." He flopped his head back down. "You've been dreaming is all."

"It was the Last Soldier," I told him. "From the Museum of Marvels at the carnival. He was here. He spoke to you."

"You read too many crazy books," Joe said. His eyes were shut, and he was already falling back into sleep.

But I didn't want to lie down. Not for a second. I sat up all night, propped against the wall, watching the door. It wasn't until the sun came up at last that I dared to close my eyes.

CHAPTER 10
SILVER BUTTONS

I wasn't sure if it was the rain that woke me that morning, or all the hollering from the kitchen. The rain pounded on our roof like lead bullets. And the cussing made the kitchen sound like the back room of a saloon bar full of drunken cowboys, not a family home above a respectable barber's shop.

For the second morning in a row I saw that Joe's bed was empty. And I couldn't help feeling an itch of worry when I saw that his new shoes had gone too.

I was dog-tired but I dragged myself out from under my sweaty sheets and went to see what all the racket was about. I reckoned it would distract me from what I'd seen, or thought I'd seen, during the night.

If Mr Gunther had had any hair left he would have been pulling it out. It was him doing the cussing. Mama was trying to calm him. But he wasn't having none of it.

"Come and see," he managed to say in between all his heffing and jeffing. "Come and see what some two-bit-good-for-nothing hoodlums have done to my shop."

Mama took her coat and held it above her head as we followed him down the stairs. The rain swept against us. After a month or more of nothing but hot sun, the heavens had burst. The street was like a river. And all that rain was blowing in sheets right through the smashed-in door of Mr Gunther's barber shop.

Mama and I gawped in amazement. We trod over shattered mirrors and broken chairs as we stepped inside.

"Who on earth ...?" Mama began. "Oh, my good Lord, this is awful. Just awful. Why would anyone do this?"

Mr Gunther's eyes burned with anger. "They've wrecked my shop, ruined my business, made me a beggar. That's what they've done."

"But why?" Mama said. "Who?"

"I found these," Mr Gunther said. He held out his hand. "Shirt buttons. They're not mine. Whoever did this must have –"

"They're Caleb's," I said. I recognised those shiny silver buttons from his smart new shirt, and I spoke before I could stop myself.

"Caleb Cubb?" Mr Gunther bit off the name in fury. "They're his? You're sure?"

I could only nod.

"All this because you rode out to see his daddy?" Mama asked. "Surely not."

"Why else?" Mr Gunther asked. "Wade says they're the boy's buttons."

I didn't want to open my mouth again, in case I'd put both clod-hopping feet right in there. They were Caleb's buttons, I knew that for certain. But I also knew he hadn't been the one who dropped them there.

CHAPTER 11
THE STORM HITS

The afternoon sky was dark, and even my bones were soaking wet by the time I reached the carnival. The roads were slick and muddy and deep with running water. I couldn't remember the last time I'd seen such a storm – if ever.

The Mitchum field was a bog. The carnival folks were taking everything down, rolling it up and packing it away. Everybody wore slickers or raincoats. They scurried through the rising mud with trunks and sacks and bags. A couple of daredevil workers in harnesses swung to and fro as they took down the Ferris wheel while the rain lashed at them. Folks were battening down the hatches like the caravans were ships in a storm on the ocean.

I was worried I wouldn't be able to find Joe. But then I guessed he might be at the gun stall. If he was planning to leave with the carnival he'd want to work that stall for sure. And this time I'd guessed right. But Joe wasn't pleased to see me.

"Go home, Wade," he said. His hair was sodden and flat to his head. I could see his face was still puffy and bruised from the beating he'd taken. "You look like you're drowning," he told me. "And I've got work to do." He was unscrewing chunky bolts with a ratchet so he could take the stall apart panel by panel.

"Come home with me," I said. "You can't just up and leave Mama like this."

"I can't come home. Not now."

"Mr Gunther found Caleb's buttons," I told him. "Why'd you do it, Joe?"

He wouldn't look me in the eye. "Because it's about time Caleb Cubb got what's coming to him," he said. "That kid needs teaching a lesson."

"But the shop," I said. "How could you do it to Mr Gunther? I've never seen him so cut up."

Joe dropped his head and rainwater flooded down his face. "It was the only way I could think of," he said at last. "I didn't want to hurt no one. No one but Caleb. Anyway, his rich daddy will pay for everything, won't he?" He nodded, as if he wanted to confirm this for himself. "Mr Gunther'll get a brand-new shop out of it, won't he?"

Joe set to work with the ratchet again.

I didn't know if it was true that Caleb's father would pay. But that didn't matter now.

"But what are you doing, Joe?" I asked. "Are you never coming home?"

"One day for sure. Of course. When I find Pa."

The wind and rain were trying to knock me off my feet and I had to shout to be heard now. "But how will you find him? You don't know where he is." And I was none too sure that our pa wanted to be found.

"I'm gonna join the army," Joe said. "That's my plan. I'm gonna be a soldier. I reckon they might be funny about my hinky arm. But only until they see how good I can shoot. I'm gonna travel with the carnival, earn my keep with them until we reach the next big town. Then I'll up and join the army. And find Pa."

"What if Pa can't be found?" It hurt to shout it so loud. "What if Pa's dead?"

Joe turned and was on me harder and faster than the rain and wind. He slammed me down into the mud and waved the ratchet close to my face. "Don't say that!" he shouted. "You say that and you're no better than Caleb. Don't you dare say it!"

He let me roll out from under him and we stood and stared at each other as the rain hammered and the wind battered the field.

"I'm joining the army to get out of here," Joe said. "Tell Mama. She'll understand."

I knew that wasn't true. Joe surely knew it too.

"Mama hates carnivals," I said. "She just wants you to come home." But I knew how lame and hopeless I sounded.

"It's my choice, Wade. Mine. Nobody's making me go. And nobody can stop me neither."

But as he said it, I knew that someone was making him go. Or some thing. The horror of it hit me like lightning stabbing down into the middle of a storm.

"No, Joe, you don't have to go," I told him. "It's the Last Soldier. He's making you go."

"Leave it, Wade." Joe shoved me away from him. "I don't have time for your stories and day-dreams. Just go, goddammit!"

"It's not a day-dream," I said. "Don't you remember last night? He spoke to you. Did he tell you to be the next soldier? I've seen him, Joe – he doesn't want to be the Last Soldier. He doesn't want to be on show like a fake mermaid or a –"

"Last soldier?" Joe shouted, his face up against mine. "What the hell are you talking about?"

I stepped back and grabbed his arm. I grabbed his hinky one so he couldn't pull away so easy. "Come with me," I said. "Tell him he can't force you. Tell him you don't want to finish up like him."

Joe pulled at his arm. "Let go, Wade, you're acting crazy."

"Please, Joe." I needed to get him to see, to understand. "Do this for me, Joe. Please."

He shook his head and wiped the rain from his face, but I could see he was going to give in. "This better not take long," he said. "I swear, Wade. You'll get me booted off the carney before we even leave Lansdale."

But I was too relieved he was following me to worry about that. I led him across the field to the Museum of Marvels, and I was glad to see it was still there at the top of the river bank. The truck trailer was swimming in mud, and the tyres were sunk into the boggy ground. I supposed that's why they hadn't moved it yet. It needed one of the bigger, more powerful trucks to haul it out of the mud. The river at the bottom of the slope behind it was a torrent straining at its banks.

Joe tried to resist when he saw where I'd brought him. I just kept yanking on his arm and dragged him up the steps before he could stop me. The old woman with the dark-eyed baby was nowhere to be seen.

But someone else was following us. Someone else was creeping through the rain.

Neither of us saw him coming. Neither of us saw the revolver gripped tight in his hand.

CHAPTER 12
THE LAST FIGHT

The rain sounded even louder inside the museum. It was like standing in a barrel while someone pelted acorns at the outside. At least it was dry. But it was darker than when I'd been here yesterday. There were no spooky lights to scare the hick customers any more. The shadows clung to the walls like thick cobwebs.

"What the hell are we doing here, Wade?" Joe asked. He ran a hand over his sopping hair and flicked away as much of the rain as he could. He sneered at the vampire bats on strings. "You better tell me right this minute or I'm –"

"This way," I said. "At the end, see?"

Joe still took his time, peering at the wolfman and mermaid and dragon as he followed me. "You know this is all hokum and shine, don't you?" he said.

"Those things all are, yes." I stood in front of the glass case and looked at the Last Soldier, screaming yet silent in his chair. "But he's not."

"What is it?" Joe asked. He bent down to read the sign. Then he shook his head. "He can't be real," he said. He got as close as he could to the glass to stare at the soldier. "He can't be."

"I reckon he is," I said. "And he followed me home. He doesn't want to be the Last Soldier. He doesn't want to spend the rest of time being gawked at with these fakes and frauds. He wanted to make me a soldier too, so he wouldn't be the last."

Joe shook his head. "You got yourself some big and hoary imagination, little brother. That's the only thing I know for sure."

I ignored him. "And last night he whispered to you in your sleep. I saw him. I did. The Last Soldier is making you join the army. You think it's your idea. But it's him. He's making you become a soldier so he won't be the last. It's nothing to do with Pa."

Joe read the sign again. "There's always gonna be more soldiers, Wade," he said. "Because there's always gonna be wars. That one in Europe won't have been the last one, no matter how bad it was. There can't ever be anything like a last soldier. He's no more true than the wolfman and mermaid. He's –"

Joe's words were lost in the din of rain as it hammered on the trailer's roof and sides. Then the trailer shuddered as a huge gust of wind shook it on its wheels, and we almost lost our balance. I put my hand on the glass case to stop myself falling.

"Why can't we let him stay the Last Soldier?" I asked. "You don't have to join the army." And as I said it, I swear I saw the dead soldier in the cabinet move, his body flinch. I whipped my hand away.

I could tell Joe thought I was crazy. "There don't have to be any more wars," I said.

But, just as Mama had said, I knew boys like Joe would always want to walk in their fathers' shoes. And men like Marshall Cubb would always say that this land, this piece of mud and dirt right here, was theirs and no one else's so keep the hell off. I heard the booming thunder outside and I felt my stomach churn because deep down I knew there would always be wars. And soldiers would always be there to die.

Joe couldn't take his eyes off the Last Soldier. He peered at the bullet hole. "You reckon this is what happened to Pa?" he asked at last. "You reckon he got shot too?"

"I don't know," I said. "We might never find out."

Joe looked from the bullet hole to the Last Soldier's face. "It's what Mama's scared of, isn't it?" he said. "She's scared she might never find out."

"She'll be just as scared if you go too," I said. "Don't you hate not knowing about Pa?"

"Of course I hate it. That's why I want to go look for him, isn't it?"

"I don't want to have to come looking for you," I said.

Joe didn't answer. He stared into the Last Soldier's eyes.

"Maybe Pa can't ever be found," I said. "No matter what."

The trailer rocked in the wind again. And a voice startled us both.

"I reckon your old man's long dead."

Caleb Cubb walked towards us down the aisle. He held a revolver out in front of him. He had it pointed right at Joe's chest.

"The whole town reckons so too," he said, "but they're just all too hoity-toity polite to say so. But if you wanna be with your dead pa, I'm gonna be more than happy to help you on your way."

I'd never had a gun pointed anywhere near me before. I felt cold and sweaty all at once. I looked at Joe. He put his hands up and I did the same.

The wind bellowed and screeched outside the trailer. Maybe the Last Soldier had flinched. Maybe he'd just been shaken as the trailer was battered so hard by the storm. I could feel the wheels sinking into the slick mud beneath us.

"It's you who put my buttons in that goddam barber's shop," Caleb said. "Admit it. Making everyone think I wrecked the place. I know it was you. Do you know what my daddy's gonna do to me if I go home?"

I saw that Caleb was scared. Angry too. But mostly just plain scared of his pa. His eyes were red and the finger on the trigger of the revolver was white. He walked closer. The barrel was aimed at Joe's heart.

"Caleb," Joe said. "Don't –"

A splitting, shrieking scream cut him off. A screech.

But not from any of us.

The trailer shuddered, shifted, twisted beneath our feet. Its whole frame tilted, tipped. Metal screamed. Metal screeched. The wheels became unstuck from the mud and the trailer slid and spun and rolled as if a giant fist of wind had pushed it down the steep bank and into the river.

It threw me off my feet and I tumbled over and over. I was hurled hard off the walls and the floor and the roof as the trailer rolled. Glass shattered. I bashed my head and rolled and smashed my leg and cried out as the world spun around me. I had blood in my eyes. I fell down on my leg, heard it crack, and felt pain bite into me. And the world crashed around me.

Joe was yelling. Caleb was yelling. I tried to yell in answer, but my breath was locked deep inside and I couldn't get it out.

The trailer hit the river water with a mighty boom and splash. The three of us thudded and tumbled and fell in a heap. At least I thought it was the three of us. But it was the battered dummy of the wolfman and the headless body of the mermaid that were crushing the breath out of me.

Water was rushing, slushing around me, pouring through the broken trailer. It churned with bats on strings and a mermaid's wig. A torn curtain snagged on the wood of a busted picture frame. A waxwork hand floated by. I was dazed, woozy, fighting not to black out. My leg yelped. It bit at me like an angry dog.

I fought for breath and coughed out Joe's name. Then louder. Louder still. "Joe! Joe!"

I was trapped. I was going to drown.

I shouted for my brother and at last Joe was there, wading towards me. He had a gash down his cheek and the darkest blood I'd ever seen was gushing out. He kept wiping it away, but the blood kept running. He grabbed me under my arms and dragged me. I howled at the pain in my leg. He grunted and I thought his hinky elbow might give up, but at last he hauled me out from under the waxworks.

I couldn't stand. "Where's Caleb?" I yelled.

Water rushed past us in the dark of the trailer. There was twisted metal and jagged glass everywhere.

"You've got to find him," I shouted. "You've got to, else he'll drown."

"I can't see him," Joe said. His face was a shipwreck. "I don't know where he is. I can't see him. He might have got out already."

Swirling water splashed up into my face and made me cough and splutter. "We can't just leave him."

But Joe wouldn't let go of me. He dragged me through the trailer, past the Last Soldier. The glass case was smashed, gone, but still he sat there in his chair, gripping his rifle, silent, screaming. The frothing, filthy river water rushed in to cover him over. It swirled into his gaping mouth.

Joe pulled me out onto the river bank. We were both shivering with cold and panic. Joe staggered but didn't fall. He had to crouch down to try to get his breath back. There were voices at the top of the steep bank and Joe waved for them to come down to help. Half a dozen carneys came slipping and sliding towards us.

"Caleb," I shouted as the rain pelted down. "Don't let him drown, Joe. You can't let him die."

Joe looked from me to the carcass of the museum as it filled with water, and I saw again the ragged, slashed wound across his cheek.

The Museum of Marvels creaked and tilted and tipped further into the rushing river. No matter how much Joe hated Caleb, he knew I was right. He nodded and waded back towards the trailer.

A pair of rough carney hands grabbed me and hauled me further up the muddy bank. But not before I saw Joe dive back into the sinking trailer.

CHAPTER 13
PA'S SHOES

Caleb Cubb wasn't the type to say thank you
to nobody. Not even to people who saved his
life. Him and Joe never talked no more, but they
never fought no more neither. And what Caleb
did do was take the blame for Mr Gunther's
barber shop. He said nothing about Joe. He just
told his daddy it was him that did it. Then he
took whatever punishment it was that his daddy
doled out to him, and his daddy paid through the
nose to fix the shop up again.

On the afternoon of the storm, the carney
folks carried me and Joe round to Doc Baxter's
house on Given Street. I think they took Caleb
straight home. He had a dint in his head the size
of a baseball, but even though he'd been out cold
and half-drowned, they said he was fine. The
doctor put stitches in Joe's cheek and set my leg,
and gave me some real doozy medicine for the

pain. So we turned out to be fine in the end too, I guess. For the most part.

Mama was polite enough at Doc Baxter's house. She thanked him for everything he'd done, and shook his hand like a real lady. But when she got us home she thundered and roared almost as bad as the storm. She scolded us for being so stupid as to go back to the carnival in such terrible weather. She raged at us for making her worry so bad. Then she cried. And she forced us to share a steaming hot bath and drink honey tea by the bucket. Joe and I didn't dare say no.

The rain and wind blew themselves out by the evening and Mr Gunther came round to see us. He said that the carneys had dragged the trailer out of the river, but the museum exhibits were lost. All except one, he'd heard. He didn't know which one. But I could guess. And if I guessed right, then part of me felt sorry for that Last Soldier.

Mr Gunther said the carney folk didn't blame anyone for what had happened, only the storm. They'd packed up and moved on. But before they left, the story went round about how Joe had saved me and Caleb from drowning in the worst storm in over a decade. Mr Gunther said everybody in town was calling Joe a hero.

Joe did his best to pretend he wasn't pleased about being called a hero.

At last we got to bed. My leg was stiff and sore but I was so tired that even my bones sagged. I didn't reckon it would take me long to fall asleep. Even so, I could tell Joe was wide awake in his bed.

"You OK?" I whispered.

"Tired," he said. "But my head's buzzing and I can't sleep."

"Buzzing with what?"

"Thoughts," he said. "All sorts of thoughts."

"Penny for them?" I asked.

"I was thinking," he said. "What with all that day-dreaming and imagining you do, maybe you should be a writer. I reckon you read so many books, maybe you should write them too. Put that imagination to good use at last."

I suppose I could have said that I didn't think what had happened had been any kind of daydream. I would have sworn on any Bible about how real the Last Soldier was. But I didn't have the energy to start squabbling. And I kind of liked his idea anyway. I don't know where he'd got it from, but a writer was something I could imagine being. I liked the idea that a book I'd written might be read by Mr Gunther on a quiet day in his shop sometime. Maybe he'd even tell his customers how he knew me before I was famous.

"But what about you?" I asked Joe. "After all that, do you still want to join the army and go looking for Pa?"

Joe took a long time to answer.

"I don't think I'd make a very good solider," he said. "I never won a fight in my life."

"You saved Caleb's life," I said. "Soldiers save lives too, don't they?"

"Maybe," Joe said.

He fell silent and I thought he was asleep. I was drifting off myself when he spoke again. "I

don't want Mama to spend every day worrying
no more," he said. "It ain't fair on her. I'm gonna
ask Mr Gunther to train me up as a barber. If
he'll let me work for him, it might be a way
to pay him back. You know, for what really
happened to his shop."

"Don't you want to follow in Pa's footsteps no
more?" I asked.

"Pa was a barber too," he told me.

At the time I didn't believe Joe would ever be
happy being a barber, but he proved me wrong.
It was less than a month later, with Mr Gunther's
shop all fixed-up like new again, that my brother
cut his first shaggy head of hair.

He looked nervous. Maybe that was because
Mama and me were sitting towards the back of
the shop watching him. I reckoned the cowhand
sitting in the barber's chair should be the most
nervous – what with Joe's jittery scissor snips
so close to his ears. But I kept that thought to
myself.

"Should I tell Joe how proud I am?" Mama
asked me in a whisper.

"Better wait and see how many ears that cowhand's got left before you say anything," I told her.

She tutted at me and jabbed her elbow into my ribs. "But I am proud," she said. "I think your pa would be too."

"Joe might not stay a barber for ever," I said.

"Maybe, maybe not," Mama agreed. "But right here, right this minute, I'm happy he feels he's doing the right thing. And that he wants Pa to be remembered in a good way."

I wasn't sure what she meant. So she pointed at my brother's feet.

Only then did I see that Joe was wearing those shoes she'd given him on his 15th birthday.

Our books are tested
for children and young people by
children and young people.

Thanks to everyone who consulted on
a manuscript for their time and effort in
helping us to make our books better
for our readers.

Also by *Keith Gray* ...

You Killed Me

Toby is a murderer.

That's what the ghost at the end of his bed tells him.

But Toby's just a boy who loves comics, and gets called a geek by his big brother. He'd never kill anyone ...

Or would he?

The Return of Johnny Kemp

"If I tell you to run, then run, right? And I mean fast."

Dan grassed up Johnny Kemp. No one else was stupid enough to mess with Johnny. Just Dan.

Now Johnny Kemp is back, and he's out for blood ...

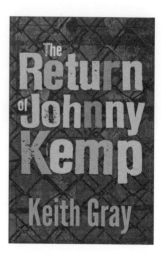

The Chain

Four people. Four stories. Four links in the chain.

Cal is sick of being the good guy. Joe's dad is a big-time loser. Ben has two girlfriends but only loves himself. Kate has to say the hardest goodbye of all.

One book, which will change their lives for ever ...

Ghosting

Nat's sister Sandy speaks to the dead. It's a gift. And a good way to make a living.

Only thing is, it isn't true.

So imagine Nat and Sandy's surprise when the dead start to speak back.

But it seems the dead are the least of their problems.